This book belongs to

This book belongs to

....

....

Written by Ronne Randall
Illustrated by Tony Kerins

This edition published by Parragon in 2011

Parragon
Queen Street House
4 Queen Street
Bath BA1 1HE, UK

ISBN 978-1-4454-3460-5

Printed in China

Before I go to sleep

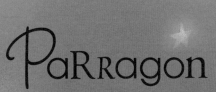

PaRragon

Bath · New York · Singapore · Hong Kong · Cologne · Delhi
Melbourne · Amsterdam · Johannesburg · Auckland · Shenzhen

Before I go to sleep,
Mommy brings my drink,
and kisses me
night-night.

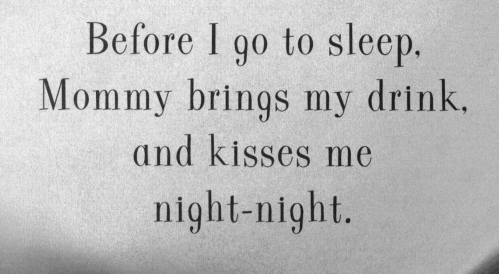

Night-night,
Mommy.

Daddy reads me a story
about the little red sailboat.

Then he kisses me
night-night.

Night-night,
Daddy.

Where is Waggy dog?

There you are.
Night-night, Waggy dog.

Before I go to sleep,
I kiss Teddy bear night-night.

Night-night, Teddy bear.
Are you sleepy yet?

Kitty isn't sleepy yet.

I wonder where
she goes at night?

Before I go to sleep,

I'll snuggle down,

and close my eyes.

Where is Teddy bear going?
Teddy bear and Waggy dog
are following Kitty.
Wait for me, I'll come too.

We'll sail away in our little red sailboat

over Grandma and Grandpa's house

and across the pond to say,

Night-night, ducks. Night-night, sky.

Night-night, moon.

Night-night, stars,

Night-night, world.

Teddy bear, are you sleepy yet?
We're almost home, now.

Night-night, me.

Night-night, you.

Night-night, everyone.

Sweet dreams